Pedal

LINDA BRADLEY

Linda Bradley

Akin House Publishing

PEDAL
Copyright © 2018
Print Edition
LINDA BRADLEY

Cover Design by Marisa Wesley of Cover Me Darling
Edited by Shauna Allen and Kimberly Dawn

Published in the United States of America by AKIN HOUSE PUBLISHING.

www.LindaBradleyAuthor.com

ISBN: 978-0-9995793-2-9

For my grandparents,
Walter and Thelma MacMillan

"Life is like riding a bicycle.
To keep your balance, you must keep moving."
-Albert Einstein

CHAPTER 1
Paula

THE CHARM OF Bay View gleamed in the grand Gingerbread architecture as it stood watch from the hills overlooking Little Traverse Bay. The sun sparkled against the water, throwing flashes of light across the shore like one of Grandma Beatrice's ball gowns on New Year's Eve. Unexpectedly, the familiar drive grounded me. I wasn't sure it would. After losing my son Charlie, I'd stayed away thinking I needed time to heal, but now that I was here, I hoped this was where I needed to be.

With the sunroof open, and the windows rolled down, I inhaled the beauty of northern Michigan. Warm light cascaded down around me. Images of Charlie trickled through the crevices in my mind. He'd loved this place more than anywhere; he'd married Tilly here and made it their permanent home.

Charlie was my oldest and had been the picture

of health. He lived for fitness and endurance. He'd fallen head over heels for the girl he'd met quite by accident in the O'Hare airport. Tilly had sat next to him while waiting for the same connection. After three hours of casual conversation, they'd found themselves sitting side by side again for the flight home. By the time the plane had touched down in Detroit, Charlie knew she was *the one* for him.

Opening their bike shop, *PEDAL,* had been a dream come true. Charlie and Tilly had been on top of the world. Business was great, and they'd begun talking about starting a family. No one had the faintest idea Charlie's heart would stop beating after a routine workout. One minute he was lacing his shoes for the ride home, and the next, he'd collapsed without warning.

Catching my breath, the bend in the road brought me upon Tilly maneuvering her bicycle up the incline leading home. Its fire-engine-red coat of paint matched her spunk. Her calf muscles were ripped with definition, and her determination was just as fierce. Leaning forward into the handlebars, she pedaled harder. Ingrained in her soul was something I'd lost. Willpower.

Tilly was a breath of fresh air. Her free spirit and generous nature lightened my mood. I knew she missed Charlie, too, but she dealt with grief differently. While she focused on the universe's Zen, I kept my sorrow bottled up and prayed like hell that someday the dull ache lodged in the pit of my belly would fade away.

Tilly's muscles flexed as she pedaled harder. Perplexed by her stamina, I thought about my own. Some days getting up in the morning took every ounce of energy I had. My role as a social worker had its perks, but listening to the world's problems weighed me down when I couldn't seem to navigate my own. And the days of feeling effective were becoming few and far between. When I'd told my office partner I was taking the summer off, she'd sighed and wished me well as if I'd packed up my desk and retired.

Tilly's blond locks fell around her shoulders as she unsnapped the strap of her helmet. Sweat lined her brow, and her damp shirt clung to her slender figure. She waved as I parked the car. Thanks to the girl who'd captured my boy's heart, the Murphy homestead looked better than ever. Her natural instincts kicked into overdrive when it came to maintaining the family property. Prevention was her motto. Besides, this was the place she and Charlie had called home. This was the place where she felt closest to him. As much as I believed saying goodbye meant forever, her bond with him lived on in a way I couldn't quite grasp. Nothing could keep them apart. She'd tried to convince me that if I opened my mind to the unfathomable, somehow, I'd be able to feel him by my side, too.

Glancing up at the pristine white lattice, I wondered if the old place had missed me. Listening hard, I imagined Grandma Beatrice humming over the creaky porch swing while Grandpa listened to Tigers baseball on the radio.

The years I'd spent raising my boys, Charlie and his younger brother Noah, seemed like a blip in time. I'd brought them here when the adoption was final. My parents thought I was nuts, but we were more than a single woman and two orphaned boys from different mothers. We'd unpacked our bags and somehow became a family our first summer together. I'd never come close to getting married, and it had always been just the three of us. We were inseparable.

My childhood sweetheart, Jack, and I had been inseparable, too. Remembering him made my heart thump. He was my sidekick, my first kiss, and the boy I'd thought I'd spend my life with. Our last summer together had been a steamy one, and I'd gotten pregnant. My heart skipped a beat when I thought about the miscarriage.

"Hi, Mom." Tilly's blue eyes twinkled as the clouds rolled overhead. She mopped her brow with a red bandana she kept in her pocket.

I waved in her direction. "Well, I made it."

My daughter-in-law's biking shoes tapped against the tiny stones lining the drive as she made her way over. "I'm so glad you're here." She tucked the damp cloth back into her pocket. "I thought maybe you'd have a change of heart."

"Not gonna lie. Halfway here, I thought about turning around and driving home. I even got off the highway, but something stopped me." Not willing to give Tilly an opportunity to dig deeper, I wrapped my arms around her. She was sweaty, but I didn't care. "Thanks for keeping the old place up." I'd had it on the market before Charlie and Tilly's wedding, but when they'd expressed a desire to stay on permanently, I couldn't let it go. "I owe you the world, sweet girl."

"Hardly."

"Grandma Beatrice would be proud. She would've rolled over in her grave if I'd sold her home." Goosebumps covered my forearms as the breeze caught the original screen door and slammed it shut.

"What do you say we head inside? I could use some water. It's hot out here already, and it's only the beginning of June."

"Got anything stronger? I'm sure it's five o'clock somewhere." Chuckling to myself, I followed on Tilly's heels as she lifted her bike up the stairs and rested it against the porch rail. For having such a petite frame, the girl was a force to be reckoned with.

"I have to say, working on the house sure has kept me from going bonkers. Last week, I planted climbing roses by the chimney. I think the neighbors are getting tired of Cora biting fresh blooms from their bushes, even if she is the sweetest Golden Retriever in the Midwest. Instead of building a fence, I thought I'd give her a garden of her own." Tilly smiled. "Besides, every time she brings me a rose, I know Charlie's near."

Her confidence bristled my desire to feel him too. "I don't know how you do it. You make everything look so easy. It's like he never died."

"Not sure what you mean?"

Maybe it was my reluctance to confront my son's death. Maybe it was the tone of Tilly's voice, but she made everything seem so damn easy. My pulse raced, and I had half a mind to get back in the car and drive home. "How can you act so normal? Getting up hurts. Going to work hurts. Coming home to an empty house hurts. Not hearing *his* voice makes me ache."

Tilly shook her head. Her expression soured. "I know it's hard for you, but it's hard for me, too." Her voice waivered. "You. Have. No. Idea. I miss him every day."

I turned away. My career as a social worker taught me how to nurture and give guidance, but dealing with myself was a whole different ballgame. I pinched the bridge of my nose.

"God, Mom, this isn't quite the reunion I planned. Maybe I shouldn't have pushed you to come."

My gaze drifted to the neighbor's yard. Tilly wrapped her arm around my shoulders and let me sob. I pulled the bandana from her pocket and blew my nose. "I'll be okay. Just give me a minute." When I'd composed myself, I looked at Tilly from beneath my lashes. "Apparently, the lack of hormones *isn't* going to help me here."

Tilly smirked. "Yeah, I hear menopause is a bitch."

I didn't know whether to laugh or continue crying so I laughed and pretended the last few tears were happy ones. "This is going to be some summer. Do you think you can stand having me around every day?"

"Yep. We're in this together."

Cora raised a brow as her tail thumped against the plaid bed she lounged on. She hung on our every word. Charlie had found her as a pup on the side of the road and when no one claimed the ball of fur, he adopted her. Within no time, she'd blossomed into a faithful companion who was beautiful inside and out—just like our Tilly.

Charlie had a way with lost creatures. Tilly believed he'd gotten that from me. We were the collectors of lost souls. Charlie preferred furry, four-legged friends, and I was partial to wayward children.

I stood on the porch and admired the beautiful surroundings. The Hanley place next door had a fresh coat of rich sienna with trim of plum, apricot, and mossy green. Nothing could match the hues of summer under the blue Michigan skies. Tilly had installed a trellis nearly the length of the house as a backdrop for her blushing roses. It was perfect, and I wondered why I hadn't done it years ago. Everything the girl touched thrived. Charlie was no different.

"Come on, Mom. These first steps will probably be the hardest, but I've got your back."

Tilly held the screen door open for me. Scents of fresh linen and antiques filled my senses as I stepped inside. The heavy oak table in the foyer shone beneath the French Provincial chandelier my great-grandparents received as a wedding gift. There was something pleasing in the curves of the wrought iron supporting the candle-like fixtures.

Tilly unlaced her shoes before kicking them off in the middle of the dining room. Her silhouette drifted away in the dim light as she made a beeline for the kitchen.

My footsteps grew heavy as I went upstairs to settle in. This summer would be more than planning beach picnics and working at the bike shop. Part of me had died when I lost Charlie, and recovering seemed impossible. I stopped on the landing that interrupted the staircase. Lace curtains brushed against my arm as the cool lake breeze welcomed me.

"I've missed you," I whispered, half-expecting someone to answer. When no one did, I took the last seven steps leading to the room where I'd spent many nights thinking about the what-if's and if-onlys.

The nostalgia of living in a home that housed my ancestors and my children preserved everything we'd experienced. All its contents, tangible and intangible, defined our family roots and who we'd become. Memories were packed away like winter woolens, and coming home meant revisiting all that had been.

A vase of Gerber daisies brightened the nightstand. The brass bed I'd slept in since childhood squeaked when I sat on the edge of the mattress. I dropped my suitcase next to my feet and caressed the quilt Tilly had insisted on buying during one of our Wednesday shopping trips in town. Tiny stitches created downy pockets of air in the white fabric. Embroidered pink roses adorned the golden borders. At the time, I thought it was extravagant, but now I cherished it because she'd chosen it for me.

A soft tune wafted through the hallway outside my door. Tilly loved her jazz. The angst knotted inside my heart began to ease, and being home was beginning to feel right.

CHAPTER 2
Tilly

I CAN NEARLY feel Mom's suffocating grief as it weighs upon her shoulders. She has an edginess. It worries me, and I don't know if being here will help. The lines at the corners of her eyes seem a bit deeper, and I imagine her weeping in her sleep as she dreams of Charlie. She pretends he's the only memory keeping her away, but I know better. In her teenage years, she was in love with a boy named Jack Masterson. I've seen the bundled letters tied in silky ribbon. I suspect he's the reason she never married. I think she cherishes his love like buried treasure, afraid to bring it to the surface for fear of losing the memories she clings to.

Although I haven't read the letters, I'm sure they were lovers. When I ask her about him, she's quick to tell one of her summer stories regarding their adventures together. The tone of her voice softens, and her eyes glimmer. I think he meant the world to her.

And Charlie meant the world to me. Charlie was my lover, husband, and friend. He was my knight in shining armor. I know it sounds cliché, but it's true.

I'm convinced Paula feels the same way about Jack, whoever he is. There's a longing in her expression, and it gnaws at me when she says his name. It's like a scene in a movie when the heroine believes her happily ever after will never come. Mom deserves a happily ever after. We all do.

I tap my foot to the beat of the jazz as I mix Sangria and prepare whitefish pâté for our cocktail hour. Chills run up my spine, and I imagine it's Charlie's fingertips on the small of my back. A deep smile emerges. The apples of my cheeks feel warm. "Hi, Babe. I'm not sure how this is going to go, but I hope with all my heart Mom can shed the burdens clouding her mind."

My gaze scans the kitchen. I see Charlie's silhouette leaning against the doorjamb. Squinting, I pray like hell he'll stay, but something tells me he's got other work to tend to.

I blow him a kiss. "Love you. Forever and always."

Cora brushes up against my leg. Her soft fur tickles my skin. She lets out a woof then pads over to sniff the baseboards. Her ears perk up, and her nose twitches as she peers toward the archway into the dining room. Smiling, I pour myself a glass of wine. There's no doubt in my mind, she sees Charlie, too.

CHAPTER 3
Paula

I TOLD MYSELF I wasn't going to open *that* drawer just yet, but it beckoned to me. Staying away proved impossible. Not a chance. Like I'd said before, when you've lived in a house that's created your very essence, it's impossible to avoid the things that've molded you.

Far beneath baby pictures, family photos, and locks of mahogany tresses my mother snipped from my mane at the age of three was a bundle of letters from Jack. He called to me like whispers in the night on the cool northern breeze. We both believed in soulmates, and when we met as children, our hearts beat as one. Closing my eyes, Jack's image drifted by. A hard knot formed at the back of my throat. *If only, Jack Masterson. If only.*

Memorabilia served as documentation of who I was on the outside and what I harbored within. Always had, always would. I caressed the spine of my cracked leather diary. Time had worn the cover, but not the contents. My mind tugged at tiny threads unraveling the past. I brought the book to my chest. The keepsake I treasured smelled like summer, and the power it held provoked emotion.

Shards of shame stung me as skeletons surfaced. Jack was more than a skeleton, he was real and so was the baby that almost was, even if it was years ago. Jack's life had been planned, and I'd kept the pregnancy to myself. Little did I know guilt would become its close companion. It seemed senseless to scold myself now, but thinking about what could have been compounded the losses I'd endured.

The silver locket holding Jack's picture slipped into my hand as I untied the white ribbon from the bulging journal. Peering through my reading glasses, I skimmed the pages. Each one dated neatly in the upper right-hand corner. Each one chronicling summer adventures. He'd understood me in a way that no one else ever could.

I'd spent hours beneath the covers penning my time with Jack to the tune of singing crickets. It was the only music I needed. I could feel the weight of the soft percale sheets against the crown of my head while scribing precious thoughts by the shine of the flashlight I'd hidden beneath my pillow.

Smudged chocolate tarnished the last page of heavy linen paper. The scent of coconut oil drifted up from one of Jack's notes, telling me to meet him by the bandstand. I carefully unfolded it, expecting magic dust to rise before me.

Jack's smile lifted from the matte photo framed in silver and hung in the air between us. I sighed, remembering the day we said goodbye. "If there was ever a time I needed you. . ." Tears pooled at the corners of my eyes.

I closed the locket, folded up the note, then shut the diary. Something stopped me from putting it back beneath the menagerie of memorabilia. Carefully, I placed it on top of the heap in the drawer and pushed it shut. Believing Jack was where he needed to be, and Charlie was too, I ignored the dull throb in my heart that I'd learned to live with. Staring at the tatted linen cross lying on the dresser, I said a prayer. Charlie's smile came alive as my fingers caressed the antique frame holding a picture of him and Noah. My recollection of taking the photograph. . .vivid. The day had been perfect. Unforgettable.

Charlie's fair skin freckled, but Noah's tanned beautifully, and the twinkle in both of their eyes was a beacon of life that came to me in the most peculiar way. They tried my patience then stole my heart with toothless smiles, corny jokes, and bear hugs. The beginning was rough, but like a rising stream, love overflowed into my lonely meadow.

Who would've thought I'd have to bury my son? It wasn't supposed to happen this way. Children were meant to outlive their parents.

Tilly's hum echoed in the hallway as she scurried about. I should've been helping her with the laundry, but I had my rituals, too.

"Mom, are you okay in there?"

Facing Tilly, I still wondered how she managed to get through each day. "Yeah, I'm fine."

"You don't look fine to me." Tilly's eyes sparkled in the afternoon light. Her slightly crooked smile was as warm as her touch. "You have to start somewhere, and sometimes coming home is harder than leaving." Tilly's wisdom preceded her age.

"I suppose you're right."

"I'm glad you're here. Charlie wouldn't want you to stay away."

The sliver of truth pricked me. Turning off the light, I peered out the window and across the bay. Tilly leaned against me. Her strength was mysterious. Her courage to face each day alone amazed me. How I longed to be more like the woman who'd married my son.

Tilly believed Charlie was still here, and sometimes I'd hear her talking to him as if he'd never died. I know my boy would want me here and he'd want me to get on with life, but that was easier said than done. Coming to terms with the things I couldn't change was immense. "What would I do without you?" I asked Tilly.

"What would we do without each other?" The corner of her lip tugged upward. "Tomorrow, I'm headed to the cemetery. It's been two years, but I think you know that."

Feeling vulnerable threw me for a loop, but I had to embrace the challenge if I wanted to get past daunting circumstances. I'd advised my clients numerous times to face obstacles head on, but now that I was on the other side of the table, I doubted my expertise.

The northern Michigan landscape stroked my love for a boy I'd met by chance and was lucky enough to call my son. Mother Nature's beauty magnified my Charlie's spirit. Like teenagers who'd carved their initials into the oak tree near Harbor Point, Charlie and Jack's love had permeated my soul in ways that couldn't be erased by life's harsh elements.

CHAPTER 4
Tilly

PAULA CARESSES CHARLIE'S headstone. She's his mother and my mother-in-law, but over time, she's become. . .Mom. Like Charlie, I was adopted too. I'm not sure where my birth mother is, and I've stopped looking. The dead ends disappoint me, so I've left it alone for now. Who knows, maybe someday I'll look for her again. Paula once told me families are made from love, not blood, and this notion keeps me content.

Paula dotes on me like I'm one of her own. She loves unconditionally. She sees the good in everyone and has a gift when it comes to guiding the downtrodden and lost. She makes a difference in so many people's lives, but I'm not sure she realizes the magnitude of her impact. I don't think she sees herself the way I do. She's given countless hours to those in need, including Charlie and Noah. Landing on her doorstep was a stroke of luck.

Paula fills her trunk with clothes and shoes because that's the part of her she can't ignore. When someone's in need, she's ready to help out. She's a superhero in her own right. Her willingness to give defines her. There aren't many children she can't reach. She's the Dr. Doolittle of social workers. Her heart is made of gold, and all those who are fortunate enough to know her are touched by a true *earth angel*.

Mom utters soft words beneath her breath. She needs space so I step away. My gaze scans the cemetery. Hazy images of women wearing ivory gowns and wide-brimmed hats adorned with flowers stroll past. Their attention focuses on something other than Mom and me. The scene elicits tranquility. Part of me dreams of walking amongst the transparent figures dissipating into the distance.

"Tilly."

I point toward a granite headstone towering above the rest. "I see women wearing full-length dresses holding parasols. Something from the early 1900s." My gaze meets Mom's. When I talk about these visions, she looks perplexed, and I wonder if she believes me. "I suppose you think that's silly."

"Not really. Just wish I was more in tune."

Mom scans the dense tree line. I know who

she's looking for. Crouching down, I brush tiny green buds from the marker next to the headstone to expose Grandpa Murphy's name. "One thing is for certain."

"What's that?"

"Charlie's never alone." My heart aches to feel his touch and kiss his lips. I force myself to smile and stop questioning why he had to go. Cora trots past and drops a red rose bud near the grave marker. She wags her tail and licks my ear. "Try to keep an open mind," I say to Mom.

"I'm doing my best." She reaches down to scratch Cora's backside. "I really am trying."

Standing up, I hold Paula's hand. "I know you are." Something doubtful emerges from behind her gaze. She wraps her arm around my waist and nuzzles me close. "I know saying goodbye is tough, but try not to think of it as permanent."

CHAPTER 5
Paula

TILLY THANKED ME for going to the cemetery with her yesterday as she fiddled with the ties on the patchwork quilt my mother had made from her father's favorite shirts. The throw was draped over the brass frame at the foot of my bed and reminded me of a man who loved baseball as much as he loved Walloon Lake. Cora brushed up against my legs and licked the back of my hand.

"I'm glad you're helping me at the shop today. My assistant, Mike, will be there. He's a great guy. Not always on time, but a hard worker. He's looking forward to meeting you."

"I don't think Charlie would mind if you sold the shop." As soon as the words left my mouth, I saw the sting in my daughter's expression. Her stubborn gaze illuminated a hint of forgiveness. I didn't know what made me say it because I knew how much *PEDAL* meant to her.

"That's the furthest thing from my mind. It was

our dream. Charlie loved the shop just as much as me. Biking is in our blood."

Tilly's iron-willed attitude reminded me of Charlie. When he wanted something, he usually got it. By the intensity in my daughter's stare, I wondered if Charlie had heard me too. She insisted he was here, and I desperately wanted to feel him the way she did. She had a gift. She had many gifts.

"Mom, I know what you're thinking."

"You've got something I don't." My insides pinched. I stroked my girl's silken hair and took in her infectious smile. "We should go." Our footsteps didn't disturb the silence held hostage in the long hallway where I once played jacks with the girl next door.

The lake breeze blew the lacy curtains away from the windowpane near the bottom of the staircase. Squinting, I wanted to see Charlie in the beams of light filtering through the white fabric swaying to and fro. I wanted to hear him. I wanted him to tell me everything would be okay.

My fingers slid from the heavy, maple banister.

Tilly held the screen door open. Her long tresses flowed over her shoulders like golden ribbons. I stepped out onto the whitewashed porch where Grandma Beatrice and I had spent many hours contemplating life. I thought about the silver locket in the drawer upstairs she'd given to me on my sixteenth birthday as we sat side by side in the antique rocking chairs eating penuche and licking our fingers. She was the one who seeded the power of dreams within me. When I needed a friend, she was there. When something was broken, she fixed it, including my heart.

Cora ran down the steps and into the yard, her tongue waggling from the heat, her jingling tags marked her hurry.

Tilly opened the car door and settled behind the steering wheel. She watched me buckle up as if I were a child then smacked her lips together in the rearview mirror. Cora stuck her snout out the back window, sniffing the air.

The scenery held my attention as Tilly navigated the winding roads through Bay View. Her eyes scanned the impeccable landscaping and Victorian architecture. Green canopies shrouded ancient oaks swaying in the breeze. I imagined the sound of a steam train coming to a halt and people scurrying through the streets to hear the inspiration of Kate Douglas Wiggin, author of *Rebecca of Sunnybrook Farm*. Grandma's signed, first edition was proudly displayed on the bureau in our living room. Tilly reached over and patted my hand, breaking the daydream.

"Mom, what would you do if you saw Jack Masterson again?" Tilly tucked blond locks of hair behind her ear. "I know what I'd do if I saw Charlie. I'd throw my arms around him and never let go."

"It's been so many years. I don't know if I'd even recognize him, and I'm not sure he'd want me to throw my arms around him. The last I knew, he lived in Sacramento with his wife and three boys." My cheeks warmed at Tilly's gaze. She knew about the stack of letters I'd saved, but it wasn't like her to have read something so personal. If she had, I didn't think she would've asked about Jack in her usual carefree manner.

"I know you wonder about him." Tilly focused on the road. "Not everyone organizes old letters in chronological order then ties them off with ribbon. He must've been something special."

"He was special all right. Summer magic and Jack Masterson were a killer combo when it came to wearing rose-colored glasses while watching the sunset." My mouth went dry, and I knew today was the day I'd tell my secret to Tilly. She'd guard it with her life just as I had.

I stared out the window, admiring beautiful hanging baskets of purple petunias as we passed the Terrace Inn. Glancing back, I thought I caught a glimpse of a person peeking out of a top-story window. I wondered if the ghost stories that surrounded the old hotel were true as her translucent profile disappeared. I turned back toward Tilly. "When Jack left for UCLA, I was devastated. He didn't know I was pregnant. No one did. I didn't know how to tell him, so I kept it to myself. Sure, we'd planned to see each other again, but then life happened. He went his way, and I went mine."

Tilly hit the brakes and skidded to a stop on the side of the road, her eyes as big as saucers. Her mouth hung open momentarily while she digested the story. "Holy crap. I had no idea." White-knuckled, she gripped the wheel.

"I've never told anyone about the pregnancy." Sniffling, I wiped at the corners of my eyes. "Two days later, I lost the baby. Part of me was relieved, and the other part of me grieved because we loved each other. In the blink of an eye, the anguish I felt quickly turned into remorse." Saying the words released manifested pressure I hadn't realized I'd put upon myself.

"I'm so sorry you had to go through that."

"Me, too." Sighing, I could see Tilly's mind churn behind her stare. "How in the world would I have managed a baby by myself?"

"You did just fine raising Charlie and Noah. They don't seem too screwed up to me."

My daughter's silly expression made me smile. She knew my thoughts on normalcy. It was all relative. "Thanks for the compliment, but I can't imagine what you're thinking."

"I'm thinking we just became a whole lot closer."

CHAPTER 6
Tilly

CORA'S SOFT PANTS tickle my cheek before turning her attention to Paula who's just bared her soul. Her secret shocks me, and I'm at a loss for words. My furry companion listens intently, her fuzzy snout resting on Paula's shoulder. Cora is the best therapist I know and a whole lot cheaper. Lord knows she's gotten me through many lonely nights.

I hold Paula's trembling hand. She's spent her life coveting lost loves and searching for a sense of belonging. When her bottom lip quivers, it breaks my heart.

Charlie and I wanted children. Trying to get pregnant seemed impossible and then Charlie died. Part of me mourns for the babies we never conceived. I picture them hovering overhead, their feathery angel wings fluttering non-stop, their hearts eager to love. But I know they're with Charlie and when it's my time, they'll greet me with more love than I could ever imagine.

Paula and I come from different worlds, but we are bound by loss.

CHAPTER 7
Paula

TILLY AND I drove along Highway 31 into Petoskey. The bay glistened like a sheet of diamonds beside us. "So, what's in store for me today? I'm not sure I'm going to be much help."

"You certainly won't be bored. The shop is busier than ever now that the summer people have returned."

Lifting my chin to the powder-blue Michigan sky, my mind drifted back to a simpler time. "A lot has changed here since I was young. I can't believe the traffic." Sunlight washed over me. The scent of sugar penetrated the air as we neared town. "Let's get some fudge today. Fudge fixes everything." The inkling to buy penuche reminded me of the woman who made fresh batches of the maple candy on special occasions. How I loved my grandmother and the time spent nuzzled into her thick bosom as she told stories about Hemingway and his antics in town.

"When Charlie brought me here, it was love at first sight." Tilly parked the car in the public lot. She took a deep breath then fixed her hair in the rearview mirror. "Northern Michigan has always felt like home, and something tells me I'll live here until the bitter end." Her concerned gaze held steady. "Will being in the shop make you too sad?"

"If you're asking me if we're going to have a repeat of yesterday, the answer is no." Unbuckling my seatbelt, I opened the door and got out of the car. Tilly peered at me through her sunglasses over the roof.

"Just checking." She slung her leather satchel over her shoulder. "Like I said, the city's not for me. Never has been."

I rolled my eyes. "Smooth, Tilly. Real smooth."

Tilly's expression reflected her zest for life. She exchanged hellos with strangers as Cora trotted happily by her side. She was as close to perfect as you could get, and if she wasn't mine I'd be irritated. Picking up the pace, I was suddenly eager to get the day started. Cora let out a woof as we paused outside Pappagallo to window shop. We were summer sisters.

"Charlie would love that you're working at the shop. Maybe we can find you a bike of your own.

Wouldn't it be fun to ride around Bay View together?"

I laughed. "God, I haven't been on a bike since college. When I graduated and left for Alma, my grandfather had given me a brand-new Shapleigh. It was blue with white trim. Plain, but sturdy like me."

"Ha. Ha. How about something red with a classic wicker basket this time? I know just where to find something like that."

"Great, are you going to get me a lap dog to go in the basket, too? Don't think your girl Cora will fit." Cora let out a throaty woof and nudged me. "Yeah, yeah. I'm not knocking your size. You're perfect just as you are. I'm the one that could stand to lose a few pounds."

"A dog? That's a great way to meet men." Tilly beamed with mischievous intent.

"I don't need a man. No, thank you." I pushed my sunglasses to the bridge of my nose. The aroma of yesteryear lingered in the air like Jack's smile at the back of my mind. I'd never met another man like him, and I wondered if Tilly would find someone she'd want to spend her life with now that Charlie was gone. I knew no one could take his place, but I was sure he'd want her to find love again. I also knew that meant accepting circumstances I wasn't so sure I wanted to. Seeing Tilly with another love just might break my heart all over again.

"You never know." Tilly shook her finger at me. "Summer magic can happen when you least expect it. What's your intuition telling you?"

"It's telling me I'm getting too old for this silliness and that I shouldn't worry about finding a man. I'm perfectly content alone. Besides, I still have Noah, and he's handful enough, even at the age of thirty-four."

"Adult sons with a wild streak don't count. I think it'd be kismet if you found love."

I raised my brow. "I'm not some wild-hearted young woman looking for Mr. Right." Tilly's wicked grin unnerved me. "I think you've been watching too many Hallmark movies."

"Love always wins, Paula. I truly believe that." She shook the door as she inserted the key. "This darn lock. Sticks every time."

"I'm past my prime just like that worn lock." My attention flitted to the canopy over the front of the store that read, *PEDAL*. Pink and white flowers I couldn't name filled the window box Charlie made when they'd bought the place. The bike shop emulated my daughter's charm.

Tilly snickered at the commentary. "I beg to

differ. Anyone who can rock pedal pushers, rosy toenails, and rhinestone-studded tortoiseshell glasses is not past their prime." She shoved the key to the store back into her pocket. "Remind me to call about getting that fixed."

The shop was cool and exuded welcoming hospitality. Bikes lined the floor in all sizes, models, and colors. The display of baskets, bells, and accessories was a backdrop behind the main counter. "We didn't have all these fancy gadgets back in my day." I inspected the compasses, odometers, and riding gear. "We wore cut-offs and canvas tennis shoes, then rode until the sun went down. Those were the days."

Great-grandfather's vintage bicycle was displayed in the center aisle. I touched the hard, cracked leather seat that held secrets of his travels and adventures. Tilly rang the bell on the handlebars as she strode past to flick on the lights.

"Doesn't look like Mike's here yet. Shocker. If you give me your purse, I'll put it in the back."

I handed Tilly my bag and followed her behind the counter. Cora curled up on her bed beneath the window next to the register, her golden fur soaking up the sun. When the bells on the door jingled, she sighed and closed her eyes.

A lanky man entered the shop with a young girl

who I assumed was his daughter. She pulled him toward a bubblegum pink bike with a white banana seat. Her baby blues glistened as she ruffled the streamers at the end of the handlebars and rang the bell.

I greeted them. "Hi there. Welcome to *PEDAL*."

CHAPTER 8
Tilly

"WHERE'S MIKE?" I mumble to myself. The silence of the back room magnifies my thoughts. The workbench is littered with bicycle parts, and Mike's vintage Raleigh hangs on the wall. He's refinished the pearly, sea-green paint and wrapped the handlebars with orange tape, making it look brand new. I make a mental note to see if he can find an old Shapleigh to fix up for Paula.

Opening the door to my office, I imagine Mom not finding her soulmate. She needs to find him. She needs someone to hold her hand, wipe her tears, and eat Sunday dinner with.

Turning on the light, my breath catches in my chest. I drop our purses on a chair in the corner under the poster signed to Charlie from Lance Armstrong. Caressing the ruby-red rosebud lying on my desk, I glance around, looking for my Charlie. My skin tingles with a soft sensation, and for a moment, I feel Charlie's lips touch mine. Closing my eyes, his presence fills me up.

The bells hanging on the front door jingle as I savor the moment.

Thinking about Paula's life, I want her to find love, too. The kind of love that makes her heart knock against the walls of her chest so loud she can't hear hesitation. The kind of love that gives warm kisses and unexpected surprises. The kind of love that makes her feel whole.

I hold the flower close to my chest. *I love you, too.*

Paula's words about selling the shop sit in the back of my mind. I smile to myself. *Don't worry. I'll never sell this place.* Something settles inside of me as I touch my cheek with the bloom. *I'll have a good day. I promise, even if it means spending all my energy keeping Mom in check.*

I want her to believe as much as I do. I want her to connect with Charlie. It would do her good. Tonight, I'll make sure to turn on the Hallmark Channel. Maybe, just maybe, it'll inspire her to buy the bike and open her heart to new possibilities.

CHAPTER 9

Paula

"I S THERE ANYTHING I can help you find?" I pretended I knew what I was doing. Truth was, a lot had changed in bicycles, but the concept was still the same. How Tilly remembered brand names and what made them top-notch, I didn't know. In my mind, a bike was two wheels connected to a frame that made you go.

When Charlie was young, he rode circles around me. I'd get so tired and without fail he'd yell, *just keep pedaling.* He'd said it so often, it became our catch phrase when things got tough.

"It's my birthday on Saturday, and Daddy said I could pick out a bike." The young girl in Bermuda shorts and a ruffled white tank skipped around the store, her braided ponytail bobbing up and down. "I want this one."

"My daughter, Jordan, is a bit excited about turning ten."

"There are lots to choose from," I found myself

saying as if I knew the inventory, but all I knew was the world of psychology and a practice dedicated to helping people with their problems. I knew plenty about that. And then some. "Ten is quite the milestone. Double-digits."

"We're having a party at our cottage," the little girl said. "My grandpa is here and everything. We're going to light sparklers, have confetti cake, and I get to pick the dinner." Jordan smiled up at her father, pride glowing in her big, blue eyes. "I never get to pick dinner." She planted her hands on her hips. "We're having barbeque chicken and pasta salad, the kind with the bowties."

"Sounds very special," I said.

"She's not shy." The man squeezed his daughter's shoulder. "She gets that from her mother."

"I think it's great. My name is Paula." I held out my hand. Jordan's warm touch flitted through me like a thousand butterflies with wings of silk. I peered over the rim of my glasses as I counted the number of missing teeth in her zealous smile. "This is my daughter, Tilly," I said when Tilly joined us.

Jordan's father smiled and something familiar flickered in his eyes, but I couldn't put my finger on it. "Tilly's the real bike whiz around here. She knows everything."

"You've got a great shop here. I'm Peter."

"Nice to meet you, Peter. I'd be glad to help with any questions. You can ride anything you see." My daughter's gaze brightened as Jordan inspected the bikes. Tilly connected instantly with the young customer. Her attentiveness was a sure sign that she'd be a great mother someday. My insides withered a bit, and I hoped disappointment didn't show in my face. The realization that another man could potentially fill the gap Charlie's death left raised countless questions in my mind, but how could I expect my Tilly to spend her life alone? Just as I had.

"I don't have any questions. I like the pink bike over there." Jordan pointed toward the back of the store.

"I like that one, too. It's a beauty. Came in yesterday," Tilly said.

Jordan retraced her footsteps across the showroom floor. She caressed the seat of the bike she had her eye on. Her expression drifted off.

"I think she's made up her mind," Tilly said. "Looks like she's daydreaming about adventure already. That's how it begins."

"A basket would look fabulous on the front. You could put your dolls in it." My words soured Jordan's expression, and her nose wrinkled. Apparently, I'd said something wrong.

"No dolls. I like to hunt for rocks. Not any old rocks though. Petoskey stones." Jordan patted her pocket.

"She's a master when it comes to spotting them. She's got quite the collection. All shapes and sizes. Her favorite ones are polished and sit on her windowsill at home," Peter said.

Jordan ran her hand over the bike seat as she walked around it, ogling the shining paint. "A basket *might* be nice though, *especially* if it had some white daisies on it."

Jordan's father rubbed his forehead. "She's also the master of getting what she wants and by the look on her face, I think she's decided."

Tilly rolled the bike out the door for the birthday girl to test ride as I answered the phone.

Cora raised her eyebrow at the interruption.

"Hello? It's a great day to be at *PEDAL*." Prepared to take a message as if I were Tilly's secretary, I picked up a pen and doodled on the notepad sitting on the counter.

"Mom, is that you?"

"Noah?" I leaned against the counter. It'd been weeks since we'd actually spoken. The world of texting kept us connected, but hearing his voice was a relief. Noah was my gypsy. Being on the go made him happy and gave his world balance.

"Yeah, it's me. I just wanted to know how things were going."

"Everything's fine. Tilly's helping a ten-year-old pick out a bike." I spared him the details of my ups and downs since I'd gotten here.

"Excellent. I don't want to talk to her though. I'm calling to talk to you."

"You got me. What's going on?" The tone of Noah's voice made me nervous. I wasn't ever sure what his next escapade entailed. Exploring Australia, trekking the Great Wall of China, or wrestling alligators in the Bayou. Somehow, he'd managed to make adventure into a well-paying career.

"I'm on my way up with a friend. We're in the car now. We should be there late tonight. Surprise."

"This kind of surprise, I like." I chuckled and thought about the times when *teenage* Noah would call and the first words out of his mouth were, *Hi, Mom. I'm okay, but...* "You're welcome to stay with us at the house." He groaned at my invitation. "Obviously, you have other plans."

"Yep, my friend has a cottage not too far from our place, and I'll be staying there."

Noah was an adult, and I didn't see the point in challenging his agenda. "I'll see you when you get here. Drive carefully. And Noah—" I paused as a gray-haired gentleman meandered past the front window. He seemed to be looking for someone, his profile familiar.

"Yeah, Mom?"

"I love you." Sometimes I thought I hadn't said it enough. Hearing him breathe into the phone lifted my spirits.

"Ditto," he said.

The gray-haired man disappeared amongst a group of window shoppers. The bell on the front door rang as some of them entered the store. I gave a friendly wave.

Noah cleared his throat. "Hattie's looking forward to meeting you."

"You're bringing home a girlfriend? Interesting." I raised my brow in speculation. I drew a heart on the notepad then sketched in choppy lines resembling a Petoskey stone. "Very interesting." This was a first for my boy.

"Yes, Mom. A girl. You promise to be nice?"

Taken aback by Noah's sigh of agitation, I sighed. "When am I not nice? I'll behave like any *normal* mother would."

"That's what scares me."

"Fine. I'll do my best."

"Later alligator. *Ciao bella.*"

"And Noah—" I stopped myself. "I can't wait to meet Hattie. See you soon." I hung up the phone.

The gentleman who'd caught my eye reappeared. I squinted into the sun trying to get a better look at him. His posture reminded me of Jack. Distracted by the customers in the store, I lost track of him when he'd gone around the corner. Cora raised her head at me. Her tail thumped against her bed. My pulse raced as I opened the door to get a better look.

Jordan rang the bell on the handlebars of her new bike as she pedaled toward the shop. "It's perfect." Her jack-o-lantern smile shone brighter than the sun.

"You're right about that," Tilly said.

She and I stood side by side. Jordan's joy crept through my veins like the calming sway of beach water. My daughter's eyes flickered with life as she spoke to Jordan's father. "What do you think?"

"I think I'm outvoted here, but it doesn't matter because I think it's perfect, too. Happy birthday, Peanut." Peter produced a credit card from his back pocket.

Jordan giggled and rang the bell three times. "Happy birthday to me. Thanks, Dad! Mom's gonna love it."

Peter nodded and rolled the bike inside after Jordan jumped from the seat with excitement. "Dad, can we get penuche when we're done here?" The sun cascaded around her head like a halo.

"Sure. I wouldn't mind a little fudge myself."

"My favorite," I said. Memories of Jack surfaced on the crest of a wave at the back of my mind. Getting fudge and sitting on the shore at sunset was the perfect way to end the day. My gaze scanned the tourists lining the sidewalk.

"Grandpa's favorite, too. We should have a penuche party." Jordan clapped. "Not sure who invented that stuff, but it's puuure genius."

Cora poked her nose out from behind the counter when the gray-haired gentleman I'd seen outside entered the shop. Jordan's eyes lit up, and she ran into his arms.

"Grandpa, Grandpa, I found a bike. Not just any bike, *the* bike."

Stunned, I closed the door behind them. Cora wagged her tail as she meandered over to investigate the commotion. I stared at Jordan's grandfather. I couldn't believe my eyes. It was Jack.

"That didn't take long," he said.

"I guess I'm a girl who knows what she wants."

I swallowed the lump at the back of my throat. My chest heaved with profound possibility. My body went numb. The world around me faded into the background as the boy I never stopped loving stood before me. I forced myself to breathe. I was speechless, and I was never speechless. I hoped like hell my eyes weren't playing tricks on me.

CHAPTER 10
Tilly

WHEN THE COLOR drains from Mom's face, time stands still. I see the look in her eyes as she greets the gray-haired gentleman holding Jordan. Peter sees what I see and tucks the receipt in his pocket. Something draws the corner of his mouth downward as he watches the scene unfold. Unsure if Mom is okay, I step out from behind the counter and it dawns on me. Jordan's grandfather is Jack Masterson. *Mom's* Jack Masterson. I glance over to Peter who seems to be dazed and tongue-tied.

"Your mother is Paula Jane Murphy?"

I nod. "Yep, she's my mother-in-law. And your father is Jack Masterson?" My words are barely audible as I observe Jordan's reaction as she sits on her grandfather's hip watching the exchange between long-lost friends.

Peter nods back, and we resemble a couple of bobbleheads on the dashboard of a slow-moving vehicle. He begins to speak then stops to rub his clean-shaven jawline. I stand quietly and wait for him to say something. "I don't believe it. Dad's mentioned her several times since he's gotten here. He certainly hasn't been at a loss for childhood stories."

I tuck my hands behind my back and cross my fingers. Something soft grazes my shoulder. I can't see Charlie, but I know he's standing behind me. The image of his smiling face drifts through my thoughts, his dimples as deep as my love for him. My heart beats for Paula, and I hope hers is thumping as madly as mine.

CHAPTER 11
Paula

MY HANDS SHOOK as the hair stood up on the nape of my neck. "Jack." Saying his name released the hitch in my chest and allowed me to breathe again. I searched his face for the boy I once knew. "I can't believe you're here." Trying to get my bearings, I stared through narrow slits over the rim of my rectangular readers.

He stepped closer, and his eyes explored mine. My heart beat faster when the curve of his mouth curled upward.

"It's been a while." He put his granddaughter down, and she scooted over to the counter next to her dad.

Tilly's brow knit together when she heard me say Jack's name. I thought about how she said she'd wrap her arms around Charlie and never let him go. Jack stood before me, and as much as I wanted to throw my arms around him, I knew I couldn't.

An invisible force filled the silence between us. "It's good to see you." Just this morning, I'd caressed his face framed neatly in my locket. His musky scent lingered amongst the ticket stubs I'd saved from the Gaslight Cinema.

Jack reached out, and I rested my hands in his. He squeezed my fingers tight. His touch took my breath away and fanned the smolder I'd refused to douse.

The young man I'd spent so many nights reminiscing about as Grandma Beatrice and I rocked together on the porch, lulling my heartache to sleep in the dark northern Michigan night, was standing before me. Neither of us was young anymore, but my rush of emotion seemed no different.

"Well, I guess you've met my son and his daughter, Jordan."

"I guess I have." I yearned to tell Jack so many things, but the audience silenced me. I glanced over to Jordan, her father, and Tilly. Peter's temple pulsated as he observed my connection with his father.

I turned back and studied Jack. The crow's feet at the corners of his eyes showed his age, but the glimmer in his green gaze personified boyish youth. His skin was as tan as ever and his touch still enticing.

Jordan skipped over and stood between us. She peered up into her grandfather's eyes. "Do you guys know each other?"

Jack nodded as he spoke. "We were friends when we were about your age."

I nodded as well, internalizing the intimate details. We were more than friends. We were lovers and in the most romantic way. Back in the day, Jack's touch sent me to the moon. I dreamed about dancing across the universe on our tippy-toes, using the stars as stepping stones, his breath in my ear, his lips on my neck, and his arms holding me close. That old, teenage giddiness knocked at the door to my heart. My gaze met Jack's. "That certainly was a long time ago," I whispered.

Jordan's brow furrowed with deep lines as she thought. "Cool." She skipped over to her new bike. She dug deep into the pocket of her shorts and produced a gray, velvet pouch. She shook it as she checked the contents. "Hey, Dad, can we ride down to the pier? I need to add some rocks to my collection." She pulled a stone from the fancy sack and strolled back over to her grandfather. "I almost forgot to show you. I found this one this morning."

Jack took the stone from his granddaughter. "It's a beauty." He held it up to the light to inspect it.

"And it looks like a heart. You can keep it, Grandpa."

Jordan caressed the stone as it lay in the palm of her grandfather's hand, then she folded each of his fingers around it until it was secure in the most protective way.

"I'll keep it forever."

"You always say that."

"And I'll always mean it, kiddo." Jack winked at Jordan as he tucked the treasure safely into his shirt pocket.

I'd given Jack a heart-shaped stone when we'd said goodbye. I often wondered if he'd kept it. And now there was a young girl standing before me, handing him her heart the way I'd done so many moons ago.

Jordan's gaze flitted from her granddad to me. Her blue eyes flickered. I'd seen that look before when the best ideas were brewing behind bright stares. Tilly and Peter had crossed the room and stood near the door.

"Do you want to come to my birthday party? The more the merrier. That's what my mom says."

I couldn't help but smile. "You're very sweet."

I glanced over at Tilly.

Anticipation resonated in her stare. I was more than a mother-in-law coming face to face with her past.

"Come on, it'll be fun." Jordan grabbed her grandfather's hand. "Tell her to come to the party. She can bring Tilly if she wants. Come on. Who doesn't like cake and sparklers?"

"I don't know," I said with a stutter.

The corners of Tilly's mouth turned downward at my response. I knew what she was thinking, but I couldn't accept the invitation. Strangely enough, I saw myself walking through a series of doors, and I didn't look back.

"We'll leave the address at the counter in case you change your mind. It sure would be nice to catch up," Jack said.

"Good idea, Grandpa. It's okay if Paula and Tilly come to the party on Saturday, right, Daddy?"

"Sure. Sounds like a grand idea." Peter's gaze met his father's. Turning his attention to Jordan, he patted her head.

My stomach rolled over at the hesitancy in Peter's response. Jack stared at me as if he'd seen a ghost. And in some respects, that's what I was. My blood ran warm, and my cheeks flushed. Embarrassed, I turned away and shuffled through the pile of mail sitting on the counter. I'd dreamed about this day my whole life and now that it was here, I didn't know what to do.

Mike entered the shop, and Tilly checked the clock. With a raised brow, she glanced his way. With a nervous greeting, he sauntered past. "I'll be in the back if you need me. Didn't mean to interrupt."

"It's okay. We're having a reunion." Jordan scanned the adults standing around her. "Right?"

"I guess you could say that." Tilly's curious voice matched the interest in her bright stare.

A wave of uneasiness seemed to wash over the group of people brought together by a ten-year-old girl and her quest for the perfect bicycle. I wrapped up a package of spoke attachments shaped like ice cream cones and butterflies. "Consider this an early birthday present. I know you're going to really enjoy your bike. It was nice seeing you, Jack." My palms sweated, and I felt like a fool. It was more than nice. My insides begged me to take a chance.

I studied Jack's profile as he scrawled Jordan's address down on the pad of paper. When he left the shop, I felt like I was sixteen all over again and too afraid to tell him the truth. Cora sighed as the door closed behind him. That old familiar taste of regret soured my dismay.

CHAPTER 12
Paula

THE SHOP WAS empty, and my insides felt hollow. Cora resumed her spot in the sun beneath the window. Her gaze studied me as I ran my fingers over the address Jack had written on the notepad. Attending Jordan's party would be too hard. Jack had no idea about the child we'd lost or the love I'd clung to. I'd let him go because I had to. The things Jack needed to accomplish didn't involve a baby or a shotgun wedding. Nothing much changed. He was married, and at the end of the night, I'd have to walk away alone. Again.

Tilly busied herself behind the counter with meaningless tasks. Her posture reflected my disappointment. She cleared her throat then put her hands on her hips. "What? You're just going to pretend today never happened? Jack Masterson shows up after all this time and nothing? Unbelievable." Her voice trailed off, her eyes wide as she fiddled with a single rosebud she'd put in a vase on the counter.

Words wouldn't come.

"Mom—"

I stopped my daughter before she said anything more. My mind reeled as my heart thudded in my chest.

Tilly pointed to the workroom that'd come alive with the sounds of tools and ticking chains. "I'll just fill Mike in on today's agenda." She glanced back over her shoulder. "If you need anything, like advice or a ride to Jordan's par-ty. . .just give a holler."

The tone of Tilly's voice hit a nerve. "You know what. You said I needed a red bike with a basket. I'll take that one over there." I pointed to the front window. "Bill me, I believe you have my address." My footsteps emulated my disgust. I kicked at the stand and rolled it out the door.

"Mom—"

I shut the door behind me with a hard jerk and before I knew it, I was pedaling toward the pier. Fury fueled the adrenaline rushing through my veins. This was hard enough without my daughter-in-law's sarcasm.

Sweat streamed down my temples as my legs pumped. The breeze felt cool against my neck as I neared the shoreline. I clenched my teeth together and bore down when my legs began to tire. Seagulls squawked overhead, and in the *whoosh* of the water lapping against the shore, I heard him. I heard my Charlie for the first time since I'd buried him. His words were clear as day. *Just keep pedaling.* All that weighed me down lifted, and I pedaled harder. Tilly was right. My Charlie had been here all along.

Catching my breath, I parked my bike at the end of the breakwater leading to the classic red lighthouse at the end of the pier. I'd been visiting this place all my life. I'd stood here numerous times at sunset, listening to the sun hiss against the horizon while Jack held my hand and whispered dreams in my ear, but now it was Charlie's words giving me life. My knees creaked as I navigated giant boulders guarding the shore. Suddenly, I felt young again. Waves lapped against the side of the cement wall that sheltered moored boats. White sprays of water splashed over the side. Two young girls squealed and scampered away from something that could easily wash them into the bay.

I stood alone on the rock barrier and lifted my chin to the sun. Breathing deep, I listened. Charlie's words brushed up against me. *Everything will be okay.*

A white-haired gentleman meandered past with a cordial nod. "Fishing today?" he asked. His baggy, white pants rustled as he shuffled along.

"Nope." I pushed wind-blown locks of hair away from my face.

"Sure about that?" he asked.

"Yeah. I'm sure. Besides, I don't have a pole."

"Hmm." He scratched his whiskery chin. "Sometimes you don't need a pole."

Wise guy. The corner of my mouth lifted toward the sun overhead, knowing I wasn't the only one enjoying his antics. "Maybe some other day." I peered into the dark swells rolling from side to side with ominous intent. "Hope you catch the big one," I called out.

"Me, too." He fiddled with the box of lures then latched it shut. "You from around here, young lady?"

"You could say that."

"Thought so." His knobby fingers adjusted the line as he tied on extra weight.

"Do I know you?" I stared into the dark eyes of the gentleman resembling Popeye. My brow wrinkled.

He took a corncob pipe from his shirt pocket and tucked it between his lips. "Don't believe so, but I have one of those faces. That's what they tell me." The apples of his cheeks popped when he began whistling his sailor's tune.

Gusts of summer air caught my tunic, and I thought I'd fly away. Charlie's presence faded into the distance along with the old man's song. Something warm roused my senses in the wave of heat around me.

"Thought I'd find you here. Guess some things never change," Jack said, tucking his hands into his pockets.

My gaze fixated on the thin line where the quiet waves met the sky. My heart pounded wildly. "Sometimes they do." I turned away to hide my face.

"Sometimes they don't," he said. "Aren't you going to look at me?"

I brushed the hair away from my face and turned toward him. My stomach fluttered with nerves. I still couldn't tell him about the pregnancy. "I can't believe you're here."

"It was time."

"I can't come to Jordan's party," I said. "I saw how your son looked at me. What would your wife say?" Jack scanned the horizon then his gaze met mine. Something sad seemed to wash over him.

"My wife—" Pausing, he cleared his throat. "My wife, Sarah, has been gone five years next month."

"I'm so sorry."

"When she died, I didn't think I could put one foot in front of the other, but somehow I did. Funny how life forges on even if the ones we love don't."

I shaded my face. "Death is funny that way. As much as we want to stop living and are crippled with grief, we're forced to finish the lives we've started. I lost my son two years ago. I thought my heart would stop beating, but somehow it didn't." I bit my bottom lip. "When I come here, I imagine the days when we were young. I even find myself looking for you."

"Those were some years." Jack's cheeks flushed, and his eyes glistened like the bay.

"Which ones? The ones we spent building sandcastles or the ones we spent in each other's arms?" Surprised by my forwardness, I held Jack's gaze. I wanted to know.

"I've never forgotten you, Paula." He stepped closer. His shoulder brushed up against mine. I tucked loose hair behind my ears to see him better.

The old fisherman I'd been chatting with hollered with glee as he reeled in a healthy catch. With one hand, he held up what seemed to be a prize-winning Walleye. In the other hand, he grasped the pipe he'd been smoking. "Now that's what I'm talking about." His white hair wavered in the breeze as the sun lit his face.

"That's a keeper," I called out before turning my attention back to Jack. "You know when you're looking for something, not leaving any rock unturned, but you just can't seem to find it?"

"Yes. I believe I know the feeling."

I shook my head, thinking about the years I'd lost while on the lookout for a man as wonderful as the one who stood before me. "My son is gone. I've come to a crossroads in my career. I'm not sure what I'm even looking for anymore."

"I suspect most people spend their lives searching. Before Sarah died, she told me to live life and love again. She held my hand and reassured me it was okay to go on. As we spent our last few moments together, the thought of living without her frightened me. I loved her and the life we had. Strange how everything gets so turned upside down."

Sarah sounded lovely, and I was sure we could've been friends. My heart fluttered with Jack's heartfelt sentiments for his wife. "I'm so glad you were happy."

"Paula, your smile is as beautiful as it was when we were kids."

Heat rushed through my veins when Jack wrapped his arm around my shoulders. I felt my eyebrows arch in question.

"Do you mind?" he asked.

"How could I?" I leaned into him, staring at his profile as he gazed out over the bay. His face was fuller and his shoulders broader, but something told me, deep down he was the same old Jack.

The old fisherman reeled in another Walleye. He winked in my direction. "Looks like it's a great day for both of us," he shouted. Gulls circled overhead, scavenging for a nibble.

Jack nodded and his cheeks rosied as I answered the jolly old-timer. "Indeed, it is," I said. A wave splashed against the pier, and I squealed like a young girl at the unexpected rush of water.

The swells subsided, and Jack nuzzled me closer. "The day you said goodbye broke my heart. I was so in love with you." Something gave inside me, loosening the knots that bound me to the past.

A shadow washed over Jack's eyes. "I'm sorry, Paula. You were the last person I wanted to hurt. If it makes you feel any better, you weren't the only one with a broken heart."

"Nope, that doesn't make me feel better." I flashed him a toothy smile, trying to lighten the moment. "We were so young."

"We were more than young."

"We were inseparable." I reached up and touched his hand resting on my shoulder. "Remember how our parents used to pack picnics and we'd meet at the beach?"

"Do I ever. You were my first kiss." The wrinkles at the corners of his eyes deepened as his smile grew wider.

Squeezing his fingers, I held on for dear life as a rolling swell struck the pier. Misty droplets of water penetrated the air, and white foam threatened to soak our feet, but I didn't back away.

"We were eight," Jack said.

"I can't believe you remember."

"How could I forget? Coming up here meant more than summer vacation itself. You have no idea. Seeing you was always the best part."

I rested my head on his shoulder. "Ditto."

"On the ride up here, you were around every corner in my mind."

My heart ballooned, knowing that he cherished memories from our youth as much as I did.

"We were soulmates, Paula."

My breath caught in my chest. Validation never felt so marvelous. "Yes, we were."

"You sure you can't make it to Jordan's birthday party?" His gaze was that of a boy trying to mask a teenage crush.

"Don't you think it'd be strange?"

"Actually, I think my family would like to meet you. If it makes you feel any better, Peter and I had a good talk before I walked down here. He wants me to be happy, and if you'd come to my grand-daughter's party, that'd be a good start."

I thought about Jordan's face as she peered at me from beneath her long lashes. Her expression emulated hope just like my daughter's. "Tilly and I'll be there. My son, Noah, is coming up this weekend. I'd love it if he could meet you and your family, too. Do you mind if he and his girlfriend tag along?"

"You heard Jordan. The more the merrier."

Images of Charlie came to the forefront of my mind. The palms of his hands rested on the back of my shoulders. His touch warmed me through like the summer sun. If anyone understood the importance of embracing the unknown, it was Charlie. I couldn't help but smile. Finally, I was beginning to see the light.

CHAPTER 13
Tilly

MOM'S SITTING IN the yard wearing Charlie's Detroit Tiger's ball cap and has his favorite things spread out on the grass. The scene reminds me of one of my favorite movies, *Divine Secrets of the Ya-Ya Sisterhood*, and I shake my head at the circle of memorabilia she's created with his Star Wars figurines, Derby cars, soccer trophies, and autographed Alan Trammell baseball mitt. When she looks up, there's something different about her.

I sit in the grass and run my fingertips over Charlie's trusty compass she's placed directly in front of her. "Charlie carried this in his pocket every day. Said it would always lead him home." I feel tears sting the back of my eyes. Mom stares at me and lets me talk. "I'm sorry about what I said." She hands me her glass of wine, and I take a sip.

"I'm not." Mom words are clipped.

Wine goes up my nose, and she laughs. I hold her mischievous stare until the coughing stops.

"Nice. I finally get what Noah's always talking about."

"I save it for the finest occasions," Mom says proudly.

"I was worried. Where have you been?" I face the beautiful house I'm lucky to call home. The evening hours are upon us, and the lights glow from inside.

"I've spent the day—" Mom uses air quotes while finishing her sentence. "*Pedaling*." Mom lifts her chin and closes her eyes as if she's worshipping the heavens.

I see the red bike she hijacked up on the porch. There's no puppy in the basket, but I hear a jingling collar. When Mom opens her eyes, I raise an eyebrow in her direction.

"Thanks to you, I got more than I bargained for today." She puts her fingers between her teeth and whistles. Cora's ears perk up, and her tail wags when she sees a fluffy mutt scamper out from beneath the bushes. Mom feeds him a treat, and he climbs into her lap and licks her chin.

"Oh, good Lord. Have you lost your marbles?"

"Probably, but *he* told me to pedal, so I did."

Cora runs toward the Hanley house and picks up something between her teeth. When she returns, she drops a rose on top of the dog in Mom's lap.

Mom caresses the silky petals then hands me the fresh bloom. "I shouldn't have stayed away for so long."

I tuck the flower behind my ear. "No, you shouldn't have."

"Guess we all have to learn lessons in our own way."

"Guess so, even if it hurts."

Mom smiles. "Tilly," she says. "You're going to make one terrific mother someday."

The sun is setting, and the fireflies begin to blink in the distance. "Should I get more wine?"

Mom nods. "And maybe a snack. The penuche I had earlier is wearing off." She holds up a box from the fudge store. "Want the last piece?"

"Oh, geez." I eat the remaining crumbs then push myself up from the ground. "How long you gonna stay out here?"

"All night if I have to." The shaggy dog in her lap settles down and snuggles in.

I smile as I walk away. Grass tickles my ankles, and I think this means Mom has changed her mind about going to Jordan's birthday party tomorrow.

CHAPTER 14

Tilly

MOM AND I laugh as we stroll up the hill. The houses are lit along the way. Glimpses into our neighbors' lives bring me joy. "I'm glad we went to the birthday party. I think we surprised her when we actually showed up."

Mom hooks her arm with mine and pats my hand. "It was nice Noah could be there," she says with approval. "I like his girlfriend, Hattie. It was sweet of them to bring Jordan a gift. Hattie seems to fit right in, just like someone else I know."

"Thanks, Mom. Hattie's lovely, and I think she's good for our Noah."

Mom fingers the filigree on the silver locket hanging around her neck. "Grandma Beatrice would like her, too. Who would've thought our nomad Noah would ever find love? I guess miracles really do happen."

"Love always wins." I glance up toward the heavens. "Are you going to see Jack again?"

"Yes." Mom's dark eyes sparkle in the dusky evening light.

"Good. You two have a lot of catching up to do."

"Yes, we do." She tries to hide her smile.

I dig in my pocket, pull out a caramel brown stone, and think about the babies Charlie and I wanted. I rub the smooth rock between my thumb and pointer finger, imagining my heartbreak drifting away.

"What's that?" Mom squints to get a better view. Her vision isn't what it used to be, but I believe she's beginning to see things more clearly.

"Charlie gave this to me when I struggled with not finding my mom. It's a *worry stone*. I keep it in my pocket. I can feel his energy when I hold it close to my heart. He'll always be with me." I think about Mom and Jack and wonder what the universe has in store for them.

"I've been thinking, Tilly. There's something I have to tell you." Her breath catches in her chest and I think I see her bottom lip quiver. "I don't know what the future holds for either one of us, but if someone comes along that loves you like my Charlie, I'd like to meet him."

Mom's words please me, and I kiss her cheek. Stars twinkle as the soft clouds shift, and I make a wish. When we near the house, the evening haze toys with my eyesight. "Is that Jack?"

"Sure is."

Hope fills me to the brim. We're not watching a Hallmark movie. Paula's living one, and I have a front row seat.

Mom glances over at me.

I kiss her other cheek and wish her luck. Cora and the hound yet to be named scamper across the yard, then we go inside.

CHAPTER 15
Paula

M Y HANDS TREMBLED as I summoned the courage to tell Jack about the miscarriage. What had come back to me could easily disappear in the blink of an eye or the admission of a buried truth. Tilly kissed my cheek, skipped up the steps past Jack, and into the house.

"What are you doing here?" I couldn't imagine why he'd be waiting for me. "Is something wrong?"

Jack met me on the cobbled stone walkway.

"I couldn't rest until I came over to see you. After you left the party, Jordan said something I couldn't ignore."

I stepped closer to my childhood sweetheart. He stared at me just like he did when we were teenagers and needed to bare his soul.

His Adam's apple twitched. "If I don't do this now, I'm going to lose my nerve."

I touched my index finger to his soft lips.

"Wait." If we were meant to be together, I had to tell him. "Jack," I whispered. "There's something you need to know." My throat ached with the truth, and my insides pinched as the words passed over my lips. "I was pregnant the summer we said goodbye."

"What?" His voice waivered. Disbelief lined his furrowed brow. "Paula, no."

The palms of my hands felt clammy as I clasped them to my chest. "Yes, I was pregnant." My jaw clenched as I tried to hold steady.

"Why didn't you tell me? Where's the baby now?"

I held his hands in mine, my thumbs caressing his sweet skin. "I couldn't. Your life was planned. I didn't have the heart to derail your dreams of playing football at UCLA." My soft sniffles accompanied the crickets' serenade. "After you left, I lost the baby. I'm so sorry. I feel so ashamed."

"Oh, Paula. You should've told me."

"I know, but I couldn't. I didn't know how."

Jack's fingers trailed over my lips. My eyes brimmed with tears as I watched him walk away.

CHAPTER 16
Tilly

WHEN I PEEK through the curtains, Jack disappears into the night. Mom sits in her grandmother's rocker and rocks back and forth. . .and back and forth. She takes the silver locket from around her neck and stares at the picture inside. When I join her, she doesn't say a word, so I sit beside her and hold her hand. Her eyes flutter shut. I can only imagine what she must be feeling.

Cora nudges the screen door open and sits beside me. The ball of fur Paula brought home yesterday settles in at her feet and snores. It seems like hours pass us by as we sit in silence, and the night sky washes over us.

CHAPTER 17
Paula

THE THUMP OF Cora's tail against the porch floorboards brought me from my thoughts. Tilly patted my hand, pointed toward the drive, and called the dogs inside. Jack emerged from the shadows.

"Is it all right that I came back?"

His ironic question tugged at the seam of my lips. I nodded.

"I started to tell you something Jordan had said to me, but I didn't get a chance to finish."

I stared at him, afraid to breathe.

"I've been through a lot in my life. I think we both have. Maybe the bigger plan wasn't meant to be understood until now."

Jack shuffled up the stairs and held out his hand in my direction. I took it, and he pulled me up.

"What did Jordan say?"

"After you left the party, she sat in my lap,

snuggled into me, and asked a lot of questions about you. I asked her why she was so curious. When she answered me, she had this mysterious glint in her eye. She said maybe I was sent here to find you. She said my eyes sparkled when I looked at you."

I rested my forehead against his. I closed my eyes, and Jack kissed my lips. Leaning back, I breathed him in. He pulled out a heart-shaped Petoskey stone from his pocket.

"Is that the stone Jordan gave you at the bicycle shop?"

"No, Paula. It's the one you gave me before I left that last summer we were together." He pulled out another stone from his pocket. "This is the one my granddaughter gave me. Now I have two."

I caressed the glossy stone I'd given him years ago as a token of my love. "I can't believe you still have this." I'd given him my heart a long time ago, and I'd never really gotten it back. And now I knew why.

Jack's chin quivered as he stared at the stone in the palm of his hand. "I'm sorry, too." He tucked the rock safely into the pocket of his shirt. "I'll keep it forever. I promise."

Tilly's soft jazz wafted out through the open window. We swayed to the sultry tempo, toe to toe and heart to heart. Jack's words brushed against my skin. "Do you ever wonder what would've happened if we'd stayed together?"

"Yes." My lips grazed his ear, and his musky scent filled me up. "Once upon a time, I loved you with all my heart. That was really something. I've spent my life trying to find my way, and every time I headed in a new direction, I thought you'd be there. No one has ever come close to filling your shoes."

"I guess this time you're headed in the right direction because here I am."

My heart knocked against the walls of my chest. Soft words brushed against my earlobe, but it wasn't Jack I heard. The back of my neck tingled with energy, and I glanced over to the red bike I'd ride until the end of time. *Just pedal, Mom. Sometimes the bicycle is built for two.*

CHAPTER 18

Paula

WE'D PLANNED TO meet Jack and his family at the beach. Getting everyone organized proved chaotic. It felt like old times when I'd corral Noah and Charlie. Inevitably someone always forgot something, and we'd have to go back. Today, we'd forgotten nothing. Dollops of sunlight flickered on the dashboard as we drove through Harbor Springs, and the dogs panted in my ear. Tilly's toothy smile conveyed a fulfillment I hadn't seen in her eyes since I'd gotten here. She wasn't ready to swim in the pond yet, but seeing me do just that was like getting her feet wet. "It's the perfect beach day," I said, parking alongside the sandy shore.

"Most definitely!" She was out of the car and had the dogs situated under a shady tree before I knew it. "Hey, Noah," she called out, waving.

"Watch this." He chased Hattie into the lake and created a soaking splash beside her.

She squealed, dove in, and swam like a champ to the floating dock with Noah on her heels. He'd always swam behind his brother, too. Maybe he knew something I didn't. When they reached the platform, Noah climbed the ladder and helped Hattie out of the water. He shook like a wet hound, and she pushed him back into the lake with a hearty laugh.

I settled into the sand after I'd arranged the beach chairs along the shore. My body soaked up the heat, and I closed my eyes. I stopped. I listened. When I didn't hear the past, my spine tingled. I couldn't hear Charlie, but I knew he was there. I saw him. He was the spark in Tilly's energy. He was the joy in his brother's laughter. He was the heat warming my shoulders.

Bike bells rang behind me. Jordan called out and waved in my direction. Jack and Peter rode behind her on a bicycle built for two. Peter was on the back, telling his father to pedal. His tone reminded me of my Charlie.

After a comical dismount, Jack strode over in his Hawaiian board shorts and plopped himself down in one of the beach chairs. He wiped the sweat from his brow. "I forgot how much work it takes to ride a bike. Doesn't make it any easier when you have a squawking child behind you."

"Don't I know it." I stood up and sat in the chair beside him. Taking in the scene, it felt like we'd never been apart.

"Jordan's mom whipped up a feast. I asked her to make your favorite, fried chicken."

"You certainly haven't forgotten the way to *this* girl's heart. I'll have to thank her when she gets here." I chuckled to myself. The extra few pounds I carried didn't matter anymore. I wore the dents and scratches well, too.

Jack waved Jordan over. "I think she's got something for you."

Jordan kicked up sand as she trudged along. She wore a frilly pink and tangerine two-piece. "Hey, people." She ran the last few feet and plopped down beside her grandpa. She unzipped her beach bag and dug through the contents. "I know it's in here somewhere." She threw her shovel in the sand. "Ick, the lotion leaked." She wiped her hand on her leg. "Oh, there it is." She pulled out something wrapped in tissue paper the color of her baby blues. "This is for you, Paula. My mom told me to write you a thank you note for my present, but I like making things instead."

The tissue paper was wrinkled, but it didn't matter. Tickled that Jordan had made me something, I opened it immediately.

"I made stuff for Tilly, Noah, and Hattie, too."

I fingered the polished Petoskey stones she'd strung to make a necklace.

"I got a rock polisher for my birthday. Pretty cool. Dad drilled the holes."

"It's perfect." I undid the clasp and put it on.

"Glad you like it. Grandpa, when's Mom gonna get here? I'm hungry."

"I think she's here, kiddo." Jack pointed toward a convertible pulling into a space.

"Yay!" Jordan slipped her feet into her flip-flops and ran off.

Fingering the stones hanging around my neck, a soft breeze drifted past. The scent of suntan lotion tickled my nose. Jack held my gaze.

"Paula. . .I've been thinking."

"Me, too." My stomach fluttered. I hoped like hell we'd been thinking about the same thing and felt the same way.

"Peter's been bugging me to move back to Michigan. He doesn't think I should be living alone and so far away. I've been dragging my feet, but now—" Jack sat up and fiddled with his baseball hat. "You're here, and I don't have any reason not to. Do I?"

The sound of my heart muffled the world around me. I shook my head from side to side, not believing what I was hearing. Jack reached over and held my hands in his. "That's what I thought." He looked around to see who was watching then leaned in to give me a quick kiss.

I caressed his cheek and held his stare. "Just like old times."

"Yep," he whispered. "Just like old times." He gestured toward his son, who was unloading the car. "Remember when?"

"I sure do, but I never remember having so much stuff. I think our parents had it easy."

Peter's arms overflowed with bags and toys for the lake, but that didn't stop his wife from handing him a cooler and stacking lawn chairs at his feet.

"I think I should give my boy a hand."

Jack puffed out his chest and strolled away like he was on top of the world. Soft cheers came from behind me. I peeked around the back of the chair and raised my brow to Tilly. "How long have you been there?"

"Pretty much the whole time." She flashed her jazz hands before clapping. "Like I said before, love always wins. There's no escaping it, and I had a front row seat."

Dripping, Noah joined us while Hattie sunbathed on the floating dock. "The weirdest thing just happened. Nice necklace by the way."

"Thanks, Jordan made it for me. You're getting a thank you gift too, so be nice."

"I'm always nice." He shook his hair out like a wet retriever.

I wiped the water from my legs. "Now you know where I get it from," I said.

Tilly giggled. "Jack's gonna move to Michigan. Isn't that great?"

Noah sat down beside me and didn't say anything. If he didn't like Jack, I'd be crushed. His gaze scanned the horizon.

Tilly rested her hand on his shoulder and shook him. "Did you hear what I said?"

Noah wrapped a towel around his shoulders. "Really, that's great, Mom. It's about time someone took you off my hands!"

Tilly gave Noah a push, then she wiggled her way into his chair.

"I do like him. Stop worrying. He's a great guy, but seriously, something strange just happened."

Relieved by my boy's response, I held his stare. Tilly listened intently. She drew her knees up to her chin. Her floppy hat shaded her porcelain skin.

"I was lying out there next to Hattie, and I could've sworn I heard Charlie's voice."

Tilly smiled. "Hmmmm. What did he say?"

Noah shook his head. He buried his face in his

hands and shook his head again. "Something about telling Mom to put his compass back." He tilted his head to the side and shook it once more. "Maybe I've got water in my ears. Weird."

Tilly and I stared at each other and laughed. Noah plunked himself down in the sand and stretched out, not giving the matter another thought. Jordan ran past, kicking off her flip-flops on the way to the water, and Jack made himself comfortable in the chair beside me. As Peter and his wife, Lori, joined us, Peter glanced over the rim of his sunglasses with an approving expression.

"You were right," Tilly said, holding my hand.

"Right about what?"

"Blood doesn't make a family. Love does."

Note to Readers

Dear Reader,

Thank you for reading *Pedal*. I hope you enjoyed it. Petoskey holds a special place in my heart and inspires my writing. It's the place where my grandfather founded Camp Daggett on the shores of Walloon Lake in 1925, a youth camp that's still going strong today. It's the place where my grandparents raised their two daughters and lived for most of their lives. Visiting meant a fresh batch of grandma's penuche, walks into town for rock candy, hunting for Petoskey stones, making homemade root beer floats, playing Slap Jack, and watching the sunset from the county park. If I close my eyes, I can see my grandfather sitting in his chair listening to Tigers baseball on the radio. I can see my grandmother's grin, and remember all the things that made them unforgettable.

If you read one of my books for your book club and would like me to attend your meeting, I can be found on my contact page at www.LindaBradleyAuthor.com. Please write BOOK CLUB in the subject line. Let me know a little bit about your group, how many members you have, and what book you've read. Feel free to send me a photo. I'd love to post your smiling faces on my website. Meeting new readers is always a pleasure!

Thanks again, and I wish each and everyone one of you the energy to *just pedal* when life weighs you down.

Sincerely,
Linda Bradley

Linda's Books

Maggie's Way

"Linda Bradley's fresh voice will keep readers riveted from beginning to end. Bradley delivers a heart-warming story full of disarming honesty and beautiful drama...This one stands out!"

—Jane Porter, New York Times and
USA Today Best Seller,
Author of Flirting with Forty and It's You

"Maggie's Way is a heart-warming tale of love and loss, fear and friendship. With charming characters and a moving plot, Linda Bradley's lovely debut gently reminds us that it's never too late for second chances."

—Lori Nelson Spielman,
International Best Seller,
Author of The Love List and Sweet Forgiveness

The Romance Reviews Readers' Choice Awards – Summer 2016

Greater Detroit Booksellers' Best Award Finalist 2016

Maggie's Fork in the Road

"I loved the first book in the series. This is women's fiction with a delightful voice and cast of characters. Maggie continues her story with the same eccentric cast of characters and a new adventure to grasp. If she can just let go of her fears. I love the 'feel' of this book."

—*Susan B. James, Author of Time and Forever*

"Author Linda Bradley shows us another side...a stronger side...of a heroine I already admired. It could only get better from there."

—*Nancy Fraser, Notes from a Romantic's Heart*

Maggie's Montana

"Guaranteed to touch your heart...Maggie's Montana is a must read for women's fiction lovers. Linda Bradley's writing sings in this beautifully crafted, warm and funny story about the bonds of love and friendship."

—*Kim Boykin, author of*
The Wisdom of Hair and Palmetto Moon

"Linda Bradley's distinct voice draws you in as her misfit cast of characters wrap around your heart and take you home."

—*Roni Hall, author of Montana Wild*

About the Author

Linda's inspiration comes from her favorite authors and life itself. Her women's fiction highlights characters that peel away outer layers of life to discover the heart of their dreams with some unexpected twists and turns along the way. Her writing integrates humor found in everyday situations, as well as touching moments that make readers connect with her characters. When Linda isn't writing, she enjoys traveling, art, reading, and baking. She lives in Michigan with her husband and spoiled rescue dog, Maisey.

Made in the USA
Lexington, KY
13 July 2018